MR.MEN LITTLE MISS™

MW00946072

Daredevil
and the Super-Speed Scooter

Turn to page 32 to find out what the pictures mean!

Published by Price Stern Sloan, a division of Penguin Young Readers Group, 345 Hudson Street, New York, New York 10014. *PSS!* is a registered trademark of Penguin Group (USA) Inc. Printed in the U.S.A.

www.mrmen.com

PSS!
PRICE STERN SLOAN
An Imprint of Penguin Group (USA) Inc.
www.penguin.com/youngreaders

ISBN 978-0-8431-3321-9   10 9 8 7 6 5 4 3 2 1

"Welcome to the superstore!" said .

"How about a tickle?"

"Maybe later," said .

"We need a ."

"You should go see ," said .

"Hi, ," said .

"We need a !"

"How about this one?"

 shouted. "It is as powerful as a !"

"A ? That sounds bad," mumbled .

"It sounds great,  !"

said  . "Can I take

the for a test

drive?"

"Count me out,"

whispered. "That

looks too fast!"

But  did not hear

 . She jumped on

the 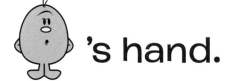 and grabbed

 's hand.

"Let's go, ," she said.

"You will *love* this!"

 pulled onto

the . Away they

went!

"Woo-hoo!" shouted

 .

"Not good, not good!"

said .

 zoomed through

the store.

"Attention, shoppers!"

 yelled. "There is a

display going on

in aisle **3**. Make that

aisle **8**. No, aisle **10**!"

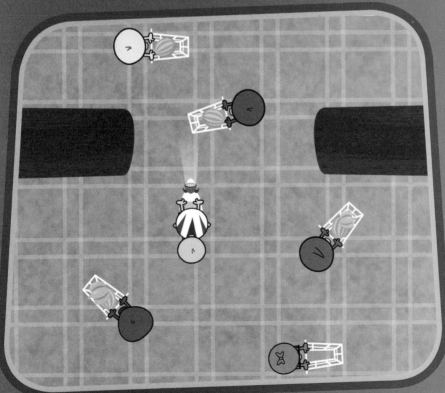

and  raced

through the aisles.

They crashed through

the  ! They

smashed into the

 !

and slammed

into a barrel of .

The barrel flew into

the air and landed on

 's head!

"Ouch!" said .

They even bumped

into  , who was

tickling a customer!

 closed his eyes

and waited for the

 to stop.

Suddenly, it *did* stop!

opened his eyes.

Right in front of him

was a giant .

"Hang on to your

patootie, ,"

shouted . "We are

going up the !"

"Not good, not good!"
 said again. He

tried to slow down

the with an ,

but the broke.

23

Next,  tied a rope

to an . Maybe that

would stop the .

But the rope broke,

too!  could not be

stopped!

drove the

up the .

and  flew through

the air. Up, up, up

they went until . . .

Bang! , , and

the crashed to

the ground.

"I am afraid I do not

want this after

all, ," said . "It

is just not fast enough."

"How about that tickle?" asked .

"No thanks, ," said . "We have some shopping to do. Come on, . We have to find a faster !"

Read along with these words.

Mr. Tickle

Little Miss Daredevil

scooter

Mr. Noisy

lion

Mr. Quiet

three

eight

ten

pumpkins

watermelons

apples

slide

umbrella

anchor